T0105558

WHAT LIES BENEATH

Mark Kevesdy

ISBN: 978-1-4269-3978-5 (sc)
ISBN: 978-1-4269-3979-2 (e-book)

*Our mission is to efficiently provide the world's finest, most comprehensive
book publishing service, enabling every author to experience success.
To find out how to publish your book, your way, and have it available
worldwide, visit us online at www.trafford.com*

Trafford rev. 09/17/2010

 www.trafford.com

North America & international
toll-free: 1 888 232 4444 (USA & Canada)
phone: 250 383 6864 ♦ fax: 812 355 4082

Introduction

Every now and then if you are still and quiet you may sense it. Not suddenly of course but gradually, that familiar yet subtle vibration softly penetrating your feet from beneath. Somewhere deep below the earth's surface, the vibration reaches you and gently sweeps over you with a soft tingling sensation. Many times you shrug it off, dismiss it from your mind and you replace it with a sudden movement of your own. But you know, as we all do, that it's there. The moment passes, time moves on, and your senses get distracted by the sights, sounds, and smells of the moment. For many, this is the routine of life these sudden movements to and from places that have no real meaning to us. We accept these regularly scheduled events as fixed place holders for our existence. Of course we have planned them with a purpose in mind yet these events never really fulfill what we desire most, to discover what really lies beneath us all. Our destiny depends on our own ability to seek truth about ourselves, humanity, and the Creator of this world. Each of us has a story to be told and yet we fear to share that story because of the lies we tell ourselves each day. Those lies prevent us from breaking our old mold and discovering the beautiful layers that lie beneath us all. Our true source of peace comes from acknowledging and accepting God's hand in all things and our willingness to be responsive to His Will for us. America once depended on Divine Providence to guide her majestic course. Lady Liberty was the true "Shining Light on a Hill" and God did indeed shed His grace on this once beautiful land we call America. But that light has dimmed. God has stopped inspiring the hearts and minds of this nation's leaders for many years. Trust in man's ability to solve problems has grown more difficult as God has slowed His response to a once God fearing people that honored and believed Him.

The destiny of America is intertwined with the destiny of the world. Those individuals whose hearts and minds are still open understand this great principle. God's freedom required a price to be paid; a price that no mortal could ever pay in this life.

Colin Madix, a fourteen year old boy from the Mid-West, accidently; yet, not coincidently discovers a world unknown to the vast majority of humans of this planet. It is a world that has the answers to America's great dilemmas. Can he respond to the call that he has been directed to?

Will the inexperience of his youth and his lack of wisdom to the things of the world be too much for him to be any factor in restoring truth and hope back into this great nation? America doesn't have much time for him to grow up and acquire worldly knowledge. His time is now or the destructive forces of nature will continue their deadly path until all is left desolate. The string of oil spills combined with fierce hurricanes has all but destroyed the U.S. Gulf Coast region. Bank failures, unemployment and foreclosures have left many homeless and desperate. Wild fires destroy thousands of acres of preserved national park land as drought continues to devastate the Western states. Terrorists from extremist groups covering all parts of the world continue their assault on America's sovereignty.

Jerusalem, a holy city to the world is under assault and no one is claiming responsibility.

What could a fourteen year old boy from the Midwest really offer the world that has already used the ideas from the best minds in America and the world to find solutions to the growing number of catastrophes but with little results?

Chapter One

It was a little after 7am on a crystal clear summer morning; the bike ride from Colin's home to the beach was uneventful. A couple of cars had passed, a jogger went by, and a woman waited for her dog to finish its business. Colin pedaled slowly across the paved road and coasted down the sandy path to the beach. He didn't bother with the kick stand and let the bike fall to the ground.

The lake was unusually calm with an occasional ripple from the gentle breeze coming from the Northwest. Colin, somewhat tall and slender, kicked the sand beneath his feet with quick strokes as if he was cross country skiing. Colin stepped up onto a fairly large rock that had been cut out from a nearby quarry. At one time the stone was part of a nearby break wall but in recent years found a new home after several violent storms off the lake.

Colin didn't think much of it, the large rock, out of place and out of purpose. It suited him fine where it was on the beach. Not meant for anything special now, but a place to sit and stare into the grey water.

Alone on the beach, Colin's thoughts drifted to thoughts of his father. His untimely death four months ago still haunted him. His mother had to pay off their farm debts selling off all of their farm equipment and the farm itself. What little they made was used to move north to Greevesport and purchase a small two bedroom Cape Cod style home with a small, fenced in yard.

~

Greevesport is a small town on the outskirts of a Midwestern city. It was a charming little town that ran along one of the Great Lakes. Several years ago, Greevesport was in the national spotlight for a famous murder trial that captivated the nation. Other than that, it remained a picturesque, postcard small town with well kept homes and yards, white picket fences, and well mannered dogs.

Colin Madix was the only child of Sarah and Eli Madix. At 14, he had only known hard work from the time he could walk. His dad would wake him up at 3:30 in the morning and say,

"Colin, the day isn't getting any longer, and we've got work to do."

His main responsibility was mucking out the barn and filling up the water buckets for his dad.

"Don't fall asleep and let the water spill over," his dad would quip.

Most of the time Colin didn't mind the work, it was one of the few times he and his dad were alone. His father stood a little short at 5'8" and had large hands that seemed a little out of place for a man his size. He was a soft spoken man, slow to anger but hard to please. Colin never quite felt his dad was satisfied with his completed chores. Deep inside Colin resented this about his father. Colin never questioned the morning routine or the assigned chores. He did them dutifully. At times, Colin waited for his father to praise him for mucking out the stalls quickly and replacing the dirty hay with fresh, clean hay, but the praise never came and Colin completed his daily tasks without every making mention to his father how he felt inside.

His mother, on the other hand, wasted no time heaping praise upon Colin or anyone else for that matter for even the smallest accomplishments.

"Thank you honey, for bringing me the canned peaches from the cellar below," she would say gratefully.

Her perpetual smile could fill even the hard hearted soul with a little warm fire inside. She was an imposing figure at 5'10" with wavy, brown hair cut at shoulder length. Her emerald green eyes seemed to penetrate every fiber of your being when she spoke to you. It was difficult to glance away from her as if her eyes held some sort of hidden force over your attention.

But maybe it was the way she spoke to you. Her words were clear and concise. Her voice never louder than what was necessary for the occasion. Colin could go to her to discuss anything on his mind.

Losing her husband and uprooting to a new town took incredible inward strength and courage on her part. After his father passed away, Colin's mother put her arm around him and said,

"You know our lives are about to change and I need you more than ever to be the young man that your father and I have raised you to be."

He remembers her tone being soft on that occasion but their seemed to be urgency in her voice. She would need to move quickly on financial matters and everything in the home and on the farm had a certain value.

"I want you to get your father's ledger and begin a list of everything we have in this house, in the barn, laying around the farm, and anywhere else you can think of to look."

He remembers doing exactly what she had told him and within three days he had created a list of over 1,000

3

items ranked from big to small. The big stuff was the easiest to list, dad's International tractor, the pick-up truck, the two 4-wheelers and so on all the way down to the number of hammers and other assorted tools.

⁓

The memory of the past four months was all present to him. There seemed to be no past and everything was in the present. It was like one day to Colin and there was not going to be a shortening of the day anytime soon.

A large sea gull cut across his vision and broke the trance. It swooped down above the water and effortlessly snatched a small fish into its talons. Colin was impressed with the bird's ability to spot a small fish from the air and glide at a perfect speed and angle to grasp its prey.

Already, the morning temperature was in the mid 70's and was expected to be in the mid 90's later that day. There was not much of breeze coming off the lake. Drops of sweat rolled down his cheek after sitting on the rock for several minutes in the morning sun. The humidity made his t-shirt and shorts feel slightly damp and Colin decided to strip down to his boxers and go for a swim. His lean body glided over the water like a surfer riding a large wave. Swimming had always come easy to him and he spent many hours swimming in the large pond on the farm.

The water still had a chill to it in early June. He guessed the water temperature to be in the low 70's and the chance for hypothermia was possible if he stayed in for too long. But with each stroke, he easily cupped the water and forced it behind him creating a small wake.

He wasn't familiar with the lakes dangerous history. It was relatively shallow, and large waves could pick up in a hurry. There was a strong cross current running horizontal to the beach about 200 yards from the shoreline. At this point, the depth drastically changed from waist deep water to a depth over 40 feet. Colin continued to move effortlessly through the water. He noticed the sudden temperature change in the water. At first, it was a quick shock to his body. But with each stroke the cold water skimmed over his body and Colin shrugged off the chill. For the first time in a long time Colin felt free. The stress of the last four months had taken its toll on him and he could feel his muscles tighten as he continued to glide through the water.

He had left his watch on the beach with his clothes. Colin was unaware of the time or how long he had been swimming. It just felt good to him and he didn't want to stop. But there were signs that he should stop and rest. He noticed his left shoulder began to stiffen on him. 'It must be the cold water,' he casually thought to himself. Then he felt his right calf twinge like when he would make a quick pivot on the basketball court. Colin may have been tall and slender, but his muscles were used to labor and the eventual fatigue that came with it.

Since the age of six, Colin had filled and carried hundreds of water buckets to the barn for the farm animals to drink. His muscle development was comparable to that of a 17 year old with an athletic build. His years of physical hard work contributed to the distance that separated him and the security of the beach. The second time he felt the twinge in his calf muscle took him by surprise. This time, without warning it came on suddenly and created a sharp burning sensation. He thrust his upper body out of the water and screamed out in agony. Grabbing his calf, he quickly massaged the leg muscle until he felt some relief.

As the pain subsided, Colin glanced around and saw nothing but open water ahead of him. It was beautiful, the glass like reflection of the water with the sun making its morning ascent. He glanced backward to estimate how far he was from the beach. The quick glance was not enough. Colin rotated his torso counter clockwise to get a better view. What he saw startled him. He could see only a small portion of the beach but to his astonishment; it was not the area that he left. This fact alone was not his main concern. The distance he swam was much further than anticipated. He remembered his dad saying the barn was 100 yards from the front porch. It was difficult to know for certain, but Colin guessed he had swum at least seven or eight times that distance, maybe more. Unknown to Colin, an undercurrent had moved Colin about 200 yards to his right or the length of two football fields. His vision of the quiet beach was replaced with a steep cliff and no beach. Colin realized he would have to swim against a current on a diagonal if he wanted to make it back to his original position. Waiting any longer would not help his situation. With his calf muscle still cramping, Colin focused on a point near the beach and began swimming again. The thought caught him off guard but it came as clear as the sky was blue that day, 'what if I don't make it back.'

Chapter Two

COLIN SWAM WITH POWERFUL arm strokes but made little progress. The undercurrent was strong and Colin felt his body begin to weaken under the strain. He lay on his back for a few minutes to regain some of his strength. While staring upwards, he pictured his mother working in the yard. The thought of her working without anyone around to help out petrified him. She was a strong person that much he knew, but if she lost both her husband and son in the same year it would be devastating. The thought of it propelled him forward from his resting position on his back.

"Come on Collin, push yourself," he said to himself.

He quickened the pace with renewed determination. His left shoulder was no longer a dull ache but now screamed for relief from the shearing pain. His calf muscle felt as if someone had punched it with their fist. Colin more aware of his desperate situation stopped again to view the shoreline.

The intense effort exerted gained him a few yards at best. A sense of dread swept over him. He hollered and waved his aching arms at the same time, "Somebody, help me!"

There was no one there to hear him. It was still too early in the morning for beach enthusiasts. Colin was alone. He felt a small wave slap him in the back of the head as it rolled toward the beach. The wind picked up making the lake water choppier. He laid on his back again. This time his body did not relax.

His left shoulder throbbed with pain and his calf muscle tightened into a twisted knot. He figured he had been in the water for less than an hour but it felt like a lot more. Another wave this time slightly larger than the last, swept over him causing him to ingest a mouthful of water. He coughed it up and projected it away from his face. Lying there, alone and little chance for rescue, Colin for the first time contemplated death. The initial thought scared him, 'would it be painful to drown?' Or 'how long would it take before he knew he was dead.' Eventually his thoughts changed as he accepted his ultimate fate.

Although he believed in a God, he did not particularly have a strong understanding of who God was or why God seemed to work in ways Colin couldn't fully comprehend. His mother and father were good, hard working people but rarely spoke about God. If God were mentioned at all, it was generally in a positive rather than a negative manner. Sometimes his dad would say to him,

"Colin, God made these animals so you could learn to work. They're not going to feed themselves so let's get moving."

He couldn't remember going to church unless it was for someone's wedding or a funeral. His mom on one occasion after his dad passed away, said,

"The Lord knows you and I need a lot of help right now but I suspect we need to use the brains he gave us to work out the predicament we're in right now."

He was raised to think for himself on religious matters. His parents offered no direction as to how he should believe. He generally accepted the idea that there must be something that was in charge of the universe. Everything seemed to have its order. The planets had their orbit. Crops had their growing cycle and humans had their growth and development. Colin really never questioned the existence of a God. But soon after the passing of his father Colin questioned God's purpose. After his father's passing, he lay awake many nights thinking about why God would allow his mom to struggle on her own without a husband. Why did God allow for a 14 year old to be raised without a father? What could possibly be gained by those left behind? At first he was angry when thinking about such questions. But soon his anger turned to sadness as he thought about not being with his dad. He tried hard not to show his emotions in front of his mom. He didn't want her to worry about one more thing than was absolutely necessary.

Now, he lay clinging to life and hiding his emotions from his mom would make no difference at all. He would be dead in a short time and nothing in his mind could stop it. A sickening thought grew louder within him, 'my mother will be left alone to bury her only child only a few months after her husband's death.' This time his body didn't have the strength to push forward. Colin had no more fight in him to stay above the water. Filled with exhaustion, Colin let his body take over. This time however, his body relaxed and sank beneath the water.

Chapter Three

THE MURKY WATER BLURRED Colin's vision to a few feet in front of him. He could barely make out the toes on his feet as his body made a slow decent towards the lake's bottom. Colin felt the tightening of his lungs as they screamed for oxygen. He knew he had taken his last breath and soon he would be dead. Waiting was the hard part. He didn't have the desire or the strength to swim towards the top for one last breath just to sink again below the surface. Instead he settled for his ultimate fate, death. It didn't take long. The murky water was crystal clear compared to the darkness that crept into his mind. He now pleaded for God to end his life so he would no longer have to endure the exploding pain within his chest cavity. 'Please God, take me now,' he thought in desperation. It wasn't long thereafter that his body became limp and his mind went blank.

A bright light descended upon Colin with a warmth and intensity he had never experienced. His body felt light.

"I am dead," he said to himself. Colin squinted into the light that was above him. He could see an outline of a figure moving within the light. He couldn't quite make out who it was but the figure was definitely human.

"Are you alright?" asked the figure above him. Colin was confused by the question. Wasn't he supposed to be asking the questions? This was after all was his first time being dead.

"If I am dead, why does my head ache so much," Colin mumbled. The figure was still over Colin and did not respond immediately to his inquiry. Colin's dull head ache didn't bother him as much as the confusion he felt inside. He still could not make out who was inside the light above him. He knew it was human and probably male by the sound of its voice. But he wasn't certain.

Colin heard the voice again ask, "Are you okay?" the figure asked again.

"Why are you asking me if I am okay?" Colin responded slightly irritated. "I am dead and everything is supposed to be fine when you are dead, right?" He asked without much confidence.

"Dead?" the figure replied.

"Are you an angel or something?" he asked.

"An angel?" the figure sounded confused.

"You know, someone sent by God to pick me up or something like that." Colin said half convinced.

"Oh, you mean a heavenly being." the figured replied.

"Well okay, a heavenly being then." Colin went along.

"No," the figure laughed slightly.

This startled Colin for a moment. He didn't fear the figure in the light but felt uneasy that his death was not as he imagined it was supposed to be. "No?" Colin's sounded perplexed.

"I found you near an opening at the base of the waterfall," the figure replied. Colin's eyes were beginning to focus better on the figure above him. The figure appeared to have hair and looked as if it were a boy about the same age as Colin. The light's intensity surrounded the figure but was not coming from the figure itself. Colin rubbed his tired eyes with his hands and then tried to sit up. He felt a gentle hand placed on his aching shoulder. "You should just lay there a little longer," the figure cautioned him.

"You still haven't answered my question," Colin asked.

"You have asked a lot of questions," the figure responded.

"Am I dead?" Colin said with a stronger voice.

"Well, no, I mean, you look fine to me," the figure spoke confidently.

"I look fine to you," Colin stated as a matter of fact. "Is there someone else here that knows what is going on or who I am supposed to report to?"

"Why don't we start with who you are?" the figure asked.

"Don't you know already?" Colin replied.

Colin felt confused. If he was dead, shouldn't his death be known to the angels or whoever else was in charge? He never thought much about what happened after one died. He did believe that life continued in some form or another. But this seemed way too complicated for him. He imagined it being similar to arriving at a train station. Someone from the ticket office would greet you and then help you on your way to your next destination.

"I only know that you look to be about my age and we are both boys," the boy replied.

Colin was seeing things clearly now. He could see the boy had brown hair cut to the eyebrows and above his earlobes. He was wearing a white robe or tunic with a deep blue sash running diagonal across his chest from the boy's left shoulder and tied at the right hip. The robe stopped short just above the ankles. He was wearing a type of sandal made of leather or a similar material.

"Ok, just answer this one question, am I dead?" Colin asked somberly.

"No," the boy responded confidently.

This was puzzling to Colin and at the same time a huge relief. Colin slowly sat up and placed his hands behind him to support his upper body.

"Here let me give you something to drink," the boy said as he lifted some kind of water container to Colin's lips.

"Thank you." Colin said appreciatively.

"My name is Benjamin."

"I'm Colin, Colin Madix."

"You look about my age," Benjamin said.

"I'm 14, but I'll be 15 in a few months," Colin added.

"I'm 14 as well. My birthday was in December."

Colin studied Benjamin more closely as they were conversing. Benjamin seemed mature for his age. He didn't have the same muscular build as Colin but he seemed older than 14 to him.

"I have so many questions like how you found me and if I am not dead than where am I and why are you dressed like that and….are you," Colin cut himself off from blurting more.

Benjamin chuckled, "you do have an inquisitive mind that is for sure. Why don't you come back to my home for lunch and we can try to answer some of your questions."

Colin hadn't thought about food until Benjamin mentioned it. He was famished. He stood up slowly and grabbed onto Benjamin's arm.

His head felt light and his body ached but other than that he felt fine.

"Sure, I'm starving," Colin said without hesitation.

Colin's eyes had adjusted to the light. He started to follow Benjamin but stopped suddenly. He could not believe what he saw.

He was so amazed at the sight before him that he stopped walking. Colin stood there staring like a young child seeing Santa Claus for the first time. Colin thought to himself, 'If I'm not dead and this place isn't heaven or somewhere in between than where am I?'

Chapter Four

BENJAMIN LED COLIN OVER terrain not unlike any that Colin had seen before. The ground beneath appeared to be the same type of dirt that was in Colin's backyard. The dirt path was wide at some points and narrow at other locations. The trees had similar green leaves like the trees near his home but appeared to have a little yellow glow to them at the tips. Colin was most impressed by the light source that illuminated the area. He could not see the sun and yet everything was bright and beautiful. It was as if everything illuminated the area with its own natural light source. There was no sky in the sense of what Colin was used to seeing. It was similar to a sky blue color but had a slight purple and orange tint as well. The sky reminded him of a beautiful summer evening sky, just after sunset over the Great Lake.

But somehow this was different. He wasn't quite sure what to make of it. He sensed he was still on earth but this place was different somehow. Everything around him seemed real enough and similar in many ways but different. He hadn't thought much about what heaven would be like. He had heard different things from friends like roads paved in gold and buildings made of jewels. But if that were true, Colin didn't want any part of it. Colin wanted to go to heaven, but roads paved in gold just seemed out of place.

He believed that there was something more than this life but what exactly that was he did not know. The idea of paths paved in gold just didn't sit well with him. If it could be anything, he thought something closer to bright green grass like on the farm but with beautiful dirt paths. Of course not a dusty dirt path that sprayed dust all over you with each step but more like crushed brick that is broken into a million pieces. He once played on a baseball field that was made of a similar material. This he thought would be perfect for a path in heaven.

Colin's thoughts drifted as he and Benjamin made their way to Benjamin's home. He worried about many things as they walked. How long had it been since he left the beach? Where was he anyway, and could he really trust this Benjamin? But he also realized that he didn't have much choice but to trust in a complete stranger. After all, Benjamin did find him and appeared genuinely concerned for his well being. Colin guessed that they had been walking for nearly an hour when they came to a beautiful waterfall. This was not like the waterfall where Benjamin found Colin. Colin estimated it was much higher than the first waterfall with the water flowing over from a height of approximately 100 feet. He had seen the Niagara Falls once while vacationing with his mom and dad a few years back. This waterfall did not have the same volume of water as Niagara but nonetheless it was quite majestic in its own right.

The sound was not like Niagara with its thousands of gallons of water pounding the surface below. The sound was more like that of a gentle spray coming from the nozzle of a garden hose. This puzzled Colin. 'How could water fall 100 feet into a pool of water below and not make a louder sound,' he thought to himself.

"This is one of my favorite spots," Benjamin declared. "What do you notice about the water?"

"Well, it is so clear and clean looking. But normally water has a greenish look to it like the pond on our farm." Colin observed. "But this water is clear but with a slight aqua blue color to it. Nothing like I have ever seen."

"Here, let me show you something." Benjamin said enthusiastically.

He reached down into the water with his hands cupped together. He began drinking the water freely without any hesitation.

"Wait; there could be bacteria in that water!" Colin blurted.

"I have drunk from this water spot for years and never once did I get sick." Benjamin reassured him. "Go ahead, try it."

Colin hesitantly moved towards the water and reached over the side of the embankment. He didn't realize how thirsty he had become. Other than a glass of orange juice early that morning, he had not had anything to drink. His body reacted quickly to the water in front of him. Without much thought, Colin plunged his head into the water and gulped it down his throat.

"Wow! That tastes like the flavored water my mom likes to buy." Colin said between gulps. "It has a slight blueberry taste to it. I have never tasted anything as delicious as this."

"I have tasted your water as well, so I know what you mean," Benjamin announced. "I'm sure you're hungry as well. There is a fruit tree just up ahead." Benjamin mentioned.

"If if is anything like this water then it has got to be incredible." Colin suggested.

"Oh, I don't think you will be disappointed." Benjamin assured him with a smile.

Chapter Five

COLIN WALKED GINGERLY ALONG a narrow path that ran alongside of a steep cliff. The path rose steadily at a 30 degree angle. Colin felt a little fatigued. He noticed Benjamin had hardly broken a sweat and had picked up a step or two over Colin. Normally, Colin would have kept pace if it had not been for the early morning swim. His body felt the exhaustion of the day's events and he needed to rest. It had been about a half-hour since the water break.

"Hey, I thought you said there was a fruit tree just up ahead." Colin expressed in an irritable tone.

"Hang in there; it is just over this ridge. I promise you," Benjamin said consolingly.

"I sure hope so." Colin said with a hopeful attitude.

They rounded a bend in the path and came upon an open, grassy field and with what appeared to be a fruit tree.

"Hold on. I'll climb to the middle of the tree and shake a couple of zapallas off the branches," Benjamin briefly explained. "They're pretty soft so try not missing them on their descent."

"Alright," Colin said confidently. Colin was impressed with Benjamin's climbing ability. Within a few seconds he was hanging over one of the bigger branches midway up the large fruit tree. The fruit tree was much bigger than the apple trees Colin was used to pruning on the farm. The fruit had a deep purple color on the outside. It was round and slightly larger than an orange. Benjamin tossed a couple more of these curious looking fruit down to Colin.

"Go ahead, take a bite," Benjamin encouraged. Without hesitation Colin's teeth sank deeply into the fruit. An incredible explosion of flavors hit the roof of his mouth and a slight tingly sensation danced around on his tongue. The juices flowed easily down his throat making the whole experience incredibly new and exciting.

"This stuff is unbelievable. I never tasted anything so good in my life," Colin proclaimed. Benjamin climbed to a lower branch in the fruit tree and then hanged dropped to the ground.

"This stuff can fill you quickly so take it easy," Benjamin said.

Colin gave Benjamin a quick glance as the fruit juice slithered down his chin and to the ground below.

"Sure, ok," Colin mumbled the words between the pieces of fruit.

$\sim$

There were very few things in life that absolutely amazed Colin. He looked at most of life had to offer with a general sense of gratitude. But the experiences of the last few hours began to weigh on him in a way that he had never experienced before in his life. There was a sense of fulfillment. A general sense of well being had taken over his anxious feelings from earlier in the day. He wasn't quite sure what it was or why exactly he was feeling this way. He just knew he was feeling different.

"I think it is time for us to move on," Benjamin interrupted Colin's thoughts.

"I feel energized again," said Colin.

"I'm glad," Benjamin replied.

The two of them were back on the path continuing the slight upward climb.

"There is a ridge around the bend up ahead that has a great view of the landscape," Benjamin said.

What seemed like another half an hour to Colin passed quickly as they moved along the path. It became increasingly harder to walk as smaller stones turned into larger rocks. Colin's feet began to ache under the constant pressure from the rocks beneath his feet. The rocks had a smooth texture to them and not jagged like the ones in his backyard. Benjamin stepped up onto a fairly large boulder and reached back with his hand to grab Colin. Colin could feel his body being hoisted up the bolder. He was impressed with Benjamin's strength.

"This is a nice view of the valley basin below. You can also see my home from here," Benjamin commented.

"Holy cow, what a view!" Colin exclaimed.

There were luscious trees for miles in every direction Colin looked. The trees were about 30 feet in height with broad pinkish blue leaves. Like the trees he had seen earlier, the tips of the leaves had a slight shimmer or glow to them. Colin observed that the leaves appeared to be giving off its own light. He not only marveled at the beauty of the trees but the apparent ability of the trees themselves to give off some kind of natural light.

"You and I have some talking to do," Colin insisted.

"Now is a good time as ever," Benjamin replied. Benjamin perceived Colin's curiosity. "I have a feeling this may take awhile," he added.

Chapter Six

THE VIEW FROM THE ridge was breathtaking. The lush trees with their glowing leaves to the aqua blue river below them; everything appeared vivid, bright, and colorful. Benjamin looked calm and peaceful. He pointed in the direction where Colin was first found near the waterfall.

"You are the first person I have ever met from above," Benjamin admitted.

"What do you mean from above?" inquired Colin.

"You wanted to know where you are, right?"

"Heck, yeah!"

"I will start from the beginning of our history." Benjamin decided. "Many years ago, during a time of great confusion and disobedience our people lived in a distant land. We were taken captive by a fierce people known as the Assyrians in ancient times."

"I remember learning about them in Social Studies," Colin shared.

"Yes, your history books do mention the Assyrians, but little reference is made about our people. Do you remember reading something about this in what you call the Old Testament?" Benjamin inquired.

"Well, I'll be honest with you; my family wasn't the church going type and all." Colin said. "Don't get me wrong about my family. My mom and dad were….well, are….I mean…, they taught me to be a hard worker and trust what God has given me." Colin assured. "We just never read much from any particular bible, that's all."

"I see. Well, I'll do the best I can with my explanation. You don't have to believe what I'm about to tell you but history can be somewhat of a messy and complicated subject. I'll just have to give you a little more background," said Benjamin.

"Just say what you have to say and I'll catch on. I did pretty well in Social Studies." Colin said confidently.

"Our people were once a part of a larger group of people known to the world in ancient times. This large kingdom was made up of many tribes and we were one of the smaller tribes. Our kingdom was united for awhile but there were differences between the tribes as to how to live and who would lead us. These differences created a lot of tension between our tribes. Sometimes we would even war against each other. But this only made us weaker and vulnerable to attack from other kingdoms."

"So you were taken captive by this kingdom known as the Assyrians because your own kingdom was not unified as a people," Colin summarized.

"Well, in some ways you are right. There is much more to the story than about unification. We were not obedient to the One who saved us from misery and death. We had rejected the One who had once unified us as a people and our people began to follow a different course of living. We rejected all that we knew to be good and replaced it with something that never brought our people fulfillment. This is the main reason that led to our captivity," Benjamin explained.

There was a slight breeze coming from the direction they had walked from that brought an added freshness to the air. It seemed fresh and even had a slight scent of flowers to it.

"That breeze felt really good. It's warm here but I don't feel much humidity," Colin assessed.

"You're right. Our temperature remains at a constant 72 degrees. It never changes," Benjamin added.

"That's like a perfect temperature," Colin said enthusiastically.

"Yes, it is perfect. But I can explain that some other time," Benjamin verified. "As I mentioned before, our people were part of a smaller tribe. My people that live here now came from this larger kingdom made up of many tribes. The Assyrians attacked the larger kingdom and took the majority of the people from the other tribes and the people that made up our tribe back to their lands. The people from the various captured tribes adapted to the Assyrian culture and lived among them. However, our small tribe did not."

"So, what happened then?" Colin asked.

"According to the history kept by my forefathers, we disappeared."

"What?" Colin sounded confused.

"We vanished from history," Benjamin said in a matter of fact tone.

"Poof, just like that. Gone from Earth?"

"No, not from Earth," Benjamin assured.

"I thought we knew pretty much about everyone. I mean to say about everyone's culture back to well, I don't know, but back to the Mesopotamians at least." Colin said.

"No, history is only a collection of information that is available to man. Many times that information is incomplete and historians have had to make their own interpretations. In other words, they have had to draw their own conclusions."

"So, you didn't really vanish from Earth but you became lost to history," Colin confirmed.

"Yes, that is correct."

"So what happened to your small tribe? I mean, where did your tribe go from there?" Colin asked with a captivated tone.

"My forefathers kept records of our journey into the wilderness. There is much written about this in our records. You can read it for yourself if you would like."

"That would be neat to read. It would be like reading Christopher Columbus' personal journal about his voyages to the American continent," Colin said in awe.

"Only better," Benjamin said with a smile.

"Ah, so you have a little sarcasm to you, huh." Colin said with a chuckle.

"Maybe just a little, I guess," Benjamin said with a shrug.

"Go on, I want to hear more."

"My forefathers tell of living in a land far away from the land of captivity. It tells of living in several lands for hundreds of centuries. But around 1,000 AD our people left these lands to the land we live in now." Benjamin explained.

"You mean, America?" Colin asked with wonderment.

"It wasn't called that then but yes, modern day America," Benjamin said.

"Oh my gosh, that would change the history books alright." Colin said sarcastically.

"Well, probably not, since history is based on obtaining accurate information about the past. And the only group that knows about our past is us." Benjamin said assuredly.

"Nobody knows about you at all?"

"Nobody!" Benjamin said emphatically.

For a few seconds this bothered Colin. He wondered why Benjamin would be telling him all of this and why would he trust Colin with all of this information. But his doubts disappeared quickly. Benjamin's explanation for his people coming to the American Continent seemed reasonable to Colin. After all, he had seen numerous television shows about lost cities; therefore, a lost tribe from the history books seemed reasonable enough.

"We came here from modern day Iceland," Benjamin declared.

"Like with the Vikings?"

"Sort of," Benjamin said." According to our forefathers, we had lived with a group of people for a short time on a large island. Our people left the group in history known as Vikings and landed on the coast of this continent. The records reveal that a great Viking explorer came searching for us but was unsuccessful. He eventually left with his search party and was never able to find us. He wasn't permitted to."

"Not permitted to?" Colin asked inquisitively.

"In other words, not allowed to," Benjamin clarified.

"Who wouldn't allow it?"

"God," Benjamin said with authority. "Our forefathers wrote about how God was preserving our people for a special purpose and we are to be obscure from the world until that purpose is revealed."

"And when is God supposed to reveal this purpose to your people?

"The records kept by our forefathers tell of a time when great trouble would be upon the Earth that will require the assistance of our people. It also tells of a young man coming to our people from the outside before the great trouble begins," Benjamin explained.

"And you think that I am that young man?" Colin asked sarcastically.

"There is no other explanation for your sudden appearance."

"But I have no idea what my purpose is for being here other than I took a swim and didn't make it back to the beach. I woke up thinking I am dead and now find myself in a world that lies beneath our own world above. Which brings me to my next question; how did I get here anyway?"

"There are openings that are only known to our people at various points around the Great Lakes in Canada and the United States. I have not been to them all but there are many. These openings can only be entered if God permits." Benjamin answered.

"So I became unconscious under water and somehow slipped through one of your openings because God wanted me to?" asked Colin.

"I believe that is what happened based on what I know from the records of our forefathers. I have seen many of these openings and it would only be possible to enter our world through the power of God."

Colin noticed the light dimming in the sky. The bluish purple sky was slowly being replaced by a pale orange appearance. He marveled at the beauty of the sky while pondering the explanation Benjamin had given him for how he entered their world. Colin felt overwhelmed but at the same time a sense of reassurance swept over him.

He felt in his heart that what Benjamin had explained was indeed true. His mind shifted to the beauty before him.

"That's interesting," said Colin. "It looks like a sunset without the sun."

"We do not rely on the sun for light," Benjamin said.

"I kind of figured that since I haven't seen the sun all day and there isn't a cloud in the sky. Yet, it is as clear and bright here; wherever that is, as it is where I live," Colin shared.

"We rely on the same source for our light as you do; it is just manifested differently here," Benjamin added. "All of our light comes from the power of God. He illuminates our days and darkens our nights. He is the source of all that we have and all that you have seen, touched, and tasted," Benjamin assured.

"I'm a little confused. What do you mean exactly?" said Colin.

"Your source for light is the sun. It lights your world, allows plants to grow, warms your days, and gives you life. Your sun came from the same source that our light comes from. That's what I mean."

"Yeah, but we have other explanations for the source of our light and plants and many other living and non-living things," Colin slightly objected.

"This is true. In your world, many facts have been distorted with time. This does explain the reason for the many explanations you have heard." Benjamin stated.

"I want to learn about your history but before we go on I have go to know one more thing, where exactly are we?" asked Colin.

"We lie beneath the Earth and unknown to the rest of the world above," Benjamin announced. "Our forefathers wrote that we were guided here by the hand of God and brought here for a wise purpose."

"So, let me get this right. We are in some underground world that is on the American Continent. Am I right so far?" Colin asked.

"Yes, that pretty much sums it up so far. You pick things up quickly." Benjamin said.

"Do I get a prize for that or something?" Colin said jokingly.

"I would say knowledge of things as they really are is a prize in itself, wouldn't you?" Benjamin replied.

"Sure, I mean, I guess so."

"We have been living under the earth for over 1,000 years. You are the only human from above to have come into our world. But I do not think this is by coincidence. The records say that a young man not from our world would be preserved for a future time and be revealed to us at a critical time in the Earth's history. This young man is supposed to be the sign from God that our purpose would be revealed."

"What? Who are you talking about? I don't know anything. I took a swim this morning and couldn't even stay afloat for thirty minutes. I don't even get straight A's in school. I mean, I'm pretty good at remembering historical facts and stuff like that but I really don't know much about the world." Colin said with determination.

"That is just it," Benjamin replied. "God works through the weak to carry out his purposes. The world thinks otherwise but the truth is the truth and cannot be changed by man's corruption."

"Are you calling me weak?" Colin said defensively.

"No, you misunderstood me. You are not weak in a physical sense but weak in the world's eyes. The world would never accept someone as yourself as having wisdom. Wisdom is a Gift from God and only those who are meek and humble can obtain it." Benjamin reassured.

"Okay so I have been led by God; although unknown to me, to your world for a purpose before a great trouble begins on the Earth. And somehow I am a sign to your people that your time is near to help our people above and the Earth itself."

"Yes"

"Okay, then how exactly are your people going to help our people and for that matter what is my role in all of this besides representing a sign to your people," Colin insisted.

Benjamin for the first time appeared anxious to Colin. It was subtle but Colin could see Benjamin begin to fidget a little. His eyes turned away from Colin's and stared into the distance.

"I think we had better move on, Colin," Benjamin said somewhat changing the subject. "I don't have all the answers to the questions you're asking but I know someone that can and would love to meet you."

"Who's that?" inquired Colin.

"My father," Benjamin said. "Let's go before it gets too dark for us to see."

Chapter Seven

THE ONCE BRIGHTLY LIT sky had slightly dimmed as Colin and Benjamin approached the cement like structure. It had four walls but they were slightly narrowed at the top where they fit perfectly with the flat roof top. The base of the structure was wider than the top. Remarkably, the structure was made up of individually cut flat stones of different shapes and sizes. The stones were flat and had an off white color to them. They were fit together tightly but without any apparent mortar or cement holding them in place. Surrounding the structure were individual stones of various shapes, sizes and colors except at the entrance. The entrance appeared to be formed with a thin layer of a translucent material unfamiliar to Colin. He estimated the structure to be about 25ft in height and 40ft in width on all four sides.

"This is my home," Benjamin stated.

"It's really cool looking," Colin replied.

Benjamin gently pushed aside the entrance door with the back of his hand allowing for both he and Colin to enter. Colin could feel the material of the door brush his back. It felt smooth to the touch like a silk blanket. Interestingly, it also had some fluidity to it. Colin noticed the door material fit perfectly into the spaces that were previously exposed to the open air. The translucent silk like door was now flush with the walls of the home. The rest of the home had simple decor and style. There were no lamps or overhead lighting that Colin could notice. Yet the inside was well lit and appealed to the eye. Colin observed the inside walls were the same stones used for the outside walls except the stone on the inside gave off light to the inside of the home.

"Let me guess," Colin said with slight sarcasm. "Your home is lit by some natural source emulating from the stone walls."

"Yes it is." Benjamin assured him. "These stones have been used for centuries in our construction. The one side of the stone has its natural color and the other side gives off a natural light. All of our buildings are constructed with these stones."

"Yes, it is the direct influence of God that makes the stone appear the way it does," a deeper voice said from behind Colin. "Sorry to startle you, I am Benjamin's father." The imposing man put forth his hand to shake Colin's hand. He, like Benjamin, was wearing a white robe of some kind with a deep purple sash over his right shoulder and tied around his left hip.

"Nice to meet you sir," Colin said somewhat nervously.

"Father, this is Colin Madix. I found him near Evans Waterfall unconscious. He only remembers swimming in the waters above and said he lost consciousness after tiring while swimming."

"I see," Benjamin's father stated. "Colin, please sit down."

Colin noticed a couch similar in form to what he had at home with the exception of the material. It appeared to be made from the same material as the door. In front of the couch was at table made from a transparent stone of some kind.

"Father, Colin has a lot of questions about who we are and where we are but I didn't feel I could answer with the same amount of detail that you could. I gave him a brief account of our history." Benjamin said.

"Well, I am sure you have a lot going through your mind right now but certainly would enjoy hearing more if you had something to eat. Benjamin, please bring us some food for all of us," his father directed.

Colin returned with three large bowls filled with various colors and varieties of plants. On top of the plants appeared to be small pieces of fish and a variety of fruits and vegetables.

"Salad," Colin said with a wide grin. "We ate salad all the time on our farm," Colin announced.

"I'm glad, you will enjoy the taste of this salad as well," Benjamin's father assured.

"Hmm, this is awesome," Colin said enthusiastically.

"It not only taste great but will keep your stomach full for hours," Benjamin announced.

The three of them ate without speaking for a few minutes until Benjamin's father broke the silence.

"You are a very special guest to us, and we are most grateful to have you in our home."

"I appreciate that, Mr. um…..sorry I don't know your name." Colin admitted somewhat embarrassed.

"Call me Eli."

Colin almost dropped the bowl when he heard the name. His face became somewhat pale.

"Why, that is my father's name as well. I mean to say it was my father's name." Colin said with astonishment.

"I know." Eli said.

"How could you possibly know that? You just met me!" Colin remarked.

"As Benjamin has probably already explained to you, our forefathers kept detailed records. In one of these records, dating back to the time our people first came to this continent, it was prophesied that a young boy from the above world would come when the Earth was in great trouble. It was prophesied that his Father's name would be Eli and he would come to the house of Eli before the great trouble would appear." Eli explained.

"What does this all mean? I don't understand my purpose in coming here other than I was somehow saved or protected from drowning. I should be dead." Colin declared.

"You are correct, Colin, you were protected by the hand of the Great One, the only true God of this Earth."

"Why, I mean, what am I supposed to do?" Colin asked aloud. "I don't have a deep religious background to speak of and I don't even know what I am supposed to do anyway."

"Your purpose is to understand your role and act upon it before great trouble appears upon this continent and the rest of the Earth. The earth is dying above. There are signs everywhere, Colin. Man has interfered with God's design and purpose for the Earth." Eli said with some sadness to his voice.

"Look, there isn't much I can do. Last year I presented a report to my science class about air and water pollution. We're just kids. I mean, we don't really have any control over what people with power decide to do with our world." Colin pleaded his case.

"The earth is dying Colin not just because of pollution in the air or water as you mentioned. It is dying because man is dying, Colin."

Colin felt powerless. He was only a 14 year old kid from the Mid-West. Pollution, crime, wars, and manmade disasters were in the news daily.

Kids wrote current events and presented them to classmates on a weekly basis. Kids make posters to hang in the hallway at school, partake in community service projects, and fundraise for various causes. 'That is all kids can really do,' Colin thought to himself. People have been creating these problems for hundreds if not thousands of years. He wasn't an adult and didn't have the means or ability to make adults change their thinking.

"So what am I to do about it," Colin asked.

"Colin, your purpose is linked with our purpose. We have a role in warning as many people who will listen about the Earth's impending destruction. Many are beyond the point of feeling God's will for them. They have died spiritually in their hearts. They are haughty and prideful. They believe the earth is theirs when in reality man was made for the earth. Man has lost their purpose long ago. They are self destructing and Earth is responding." Eli explained.

"What do you mean Earth is responding?" Colin wanted to know.

"The elements that make up the Earth have been obedient from the beginning of time. They responded to the Master's voice in the beginning and they responded to his voice when He came upon the Earth many years ago. The elements respond to goodness as well as evil. The Great One organized this planet to respond to good and evil.

The elements obey to the choices that man makes." Eli declared.

"So I am to go above and start warning people that their choices are killing the planet and eventually will kill them, is that it?" Colin said without much confidence.

"You will have help." Eli assured him.

"What, your son and I?" Colin sounded irritated.

"Colin, our world below has only a few thousand people. It has remained that way for centuries. There is a reason for this." Eli said.

He explained further. "Our people have been directed by God to live among those who live above us. Starting after the American Revolution, young married couples over the age of twenty-one, moved above ground and assimilated into the culture. They planted crops, worked the land, were industrious, had children, and raised families. No different than what you see in everyday living above ground; except there is one major difference." Eli shared.

"What is that?" Colin asked with increasing optimism.

"When the young couples reach the age of fifty-two they return to our world below and report world conditions to our people. Our life span is short. It is very rare for any of us to live past 55."

"What happens to the children left behind above ground?" Colin inquired.

"They continue their lives as normal, productive citizens and raise their own children."

"So, how do you keep the population going below ground if young married couples leave here and work above ground?" Colin asked.

"Well, not all young married couples choose to leave. Some feel the will of God in their hearts to remain below ground."

"Ok, then what about the kids born to the parents that go above ground. What I am trying to say is, how much knowledge do they have about this below ground world?"

"They are taught our history from their childhood and throughout their youth. Our culture and purpose is preserved in their hearts and minds. Although there is one thing they are not permitted to know."

"And what is that?" Colin asked impatiently.

"Where their parents have gone?

"You mean to tell me their parents just up and abandon their kids and return to this below ground world," Colin appeared alarmed.

"Their children are taught this from an early age. They are prepared physically and mentally when the time comes for their parents to leave," Eli assured him.

"I wish I were as lucky. I didn't know when my father was going to die. One minute I was helping him thin out the peach trees and the next minute he was dead. A massive heart attack killed him is what the doctors said."

"I am very sorry, Colin," Eli said consolingly.

"It just bothers me I didn't get to say good bye the way I wanted to. But what really angered me was that my mom didn't get the chance to have a few last words with him."

"There is purpose in adversity, Colin. Death makes us all more aware of our reliance on God. He is the only thing that is truly permanent. Everything else has its season. That includes you and I. Our purpose on Earth is preparing us for a life with God. There is much to learn and this life provides that opportunity. God will not interfere with that learning process even if it is a painful process. Our future after this life is the real permanence we are all seeking.

Only God knows how our individual experiences, both good and bad, affect who we are after we leave this earthly life. This is what many have forgotten above ground. They only want their needs met now with little consideration for future generations or for that matter for their own future after their life experience has ended."

"Will I ever see my dad again, Eli?" Colin asked.

"You will, Colin. That time will come when God's Will permits it. All things are accomplished in God's own time, not ours. This is what is destroying the human race. Most want all their desires met now. Their hearts are cold to God's love and timing. They have lost faith in the One who created them."

"Is it too late for humans to renew or find this faith?" asked Colin.

"Sadly, for many this is true. They have put their trust in man's solutions. They will never find it if that is where they put their trust. The solutions they are seeking to many of the world's problems are found with their trust and obedience to God. But many, if not most, refuse to believe in simple things. They have grown much too arrogant in their thinking. God has stopped inspiring man because of this arrogance," said Eli.

"So finding solutions to dying trees or cleaning oil spills is becoming more difficult because man is not receiving inspiration from God."

"That is why we had the dark ages," Eli said. "Man became corrupt in their thinking. That is why our people moved to this continent. We came here to hold onto our faith in the God of this world. We were inspired to leave and God directed our path to this world. He prepared a way for us to arrive here and had carved out this underground world before we even arrived."

"He did the same thing with the Pilgrims and others who came to this land, didn't he?" Colin asked knowing the answer.

"After the dark ages, man began to see again what they had been missing in their minds and hearts. They began to trust in God again, and in turn, He began to inspire them."

"You mean the renaissance?"

"Yes, but we are about to enter another Dark Age or possibly worse if the human race does not turn from their dangerous ways," Eli said with warning.

"What is my role then in all of this," Colin earnestly inquired.

"The records of our forefathers tell of a future time when a young boy would go among the haughty and prideful when the earth was in great distress. He would be instrumental in gathering those whose hearts have not gone cold. He would lead them back to our people below. The records tell that our people will reunite with our descendants to become a great force for good. You, Colin, have been chosen by God to bring about this work."

"When do I start and how do I get started," Colin asked with renewed vigor.

"You will leave tonight with Benjamin," Eli said with authority. Benjamin will lead you from the world below to the world above. The Earth groans with agony, Colin. There is not much time. The children of obedience must be gathered before the great destructions foretold by our forefathers destroy this continent."

"How long do we have and where do I start?" asked Colin.

"You have weeks at best and you will start with your mom." Eli responded.

Chapter Eight

It was after nine o'clock in the evening when Colin and Benjamin arrived home in Greevesport. The air was thick with high humidity and the sun was setting over the Great Lake like a giant orange sherbet ice cream scoop melting its way down into a sugar cone. Benjamin was wearing blue jeans, flip-flops, and a red t-shirt. The clothes items had been brought back by returning couples to the world below in preparation for occasions such as these.

Colin and Benjamin entered through the back screen door and into the kitchen. Mrs. Madix was putting dishes away while at the same time staring at the television. The noise from door turned her attention away from the news broadcast she was watching.

"For heaven's sake, Colin, where in heck have you been?" Sarah said angrily. "I have been worried sick all afternoon wondering where you had gone to."

"Mom, I can explain," Colin said apologetically.

"My dear God, they have done it again. We have been hit by another terrorist attack, Colin. The Capital building in Washington was severely damaged by a truck filled with explosives. The news reports coming in said terrorists are claiming responsibility. Thank the Lord you are home," she said tearfully with arms embraced around Colin.

"When did it happen," Colin asked with surprise.

"Just before seven o'clock this evening. The nightly news show was finishing a report on the wild fires in Rocky Mountain National Park when reports came in about a terrorist attack in Washington D.C."

"Who's responsible," Colin demanded.

"No one knows for certain," she said. "What is this world coming to, Colin. Every day the news gets more and more depressing. I grew up feeling safe and secure. When your daddy and I married we thought we had died and gone to heaven when we purchased the farm. Now everything seems to be falling apart. First, your daddy ups and dies. Next, we lost everything that we had worked so hard on the farm and now our country is being attacked again. I thought his death in February would be all that I would have to endure this year," she said sounding dismayed. The category 5 hurricane in May has all but destroyed much of the Florida panhandle. When was the last time we had a category 5 hurricane in May, Colin? And if this wasn't enough, fourteen F5 tornadoes have struck from northern Texas to western Ohio in the month of April and May killing hundreds and destroying homes and businesses. Their now saying the wildfires out west may destroy two-thirds of Rocky Mountain National Park and it could take weeks before they get things under control. Oh dear God, we are only in June and it has not rained in Utah, Nevada, or California in nearly 7 weeks. What is happening?" Sarah's voice trailed off as if lost in the sounds of a large storm.

"Mom, this is Benjamin. I met him near the lake today."

"Oh, I am so sorry, Benjamin, I must sound like a doomsayer," she said extending a hand to him.

"That's okay, Mrs. Madix."

"Please, call me Sarah."

"Benjamin and I have got to talk to you mom. I know things look really bad right now but there may be some hope in all of this," Colin said.

"Hun, I know you have always looked at things on the bright side, but please tell me, what in God's green Earth do you find hopeful in this?"

"Mom, please sit down for a moment," Colin said with urgency. I have a lot to say and not much time to say it, so you must believe everything I am about to tell you. I cannot go into all the details but I need for you to believe me now, mom"

"You have never given me a reason to doubt you, ever! So why would I not believe you now?"

"Okay then, here it goes," Colin said after taking a deep breath.

"Sarah," Benjamin interrupted. "I know you don't know me very well since we just met and all. But I want you to know that what Colin is about to explain to you is indeed the truth."

"Okay," she said with the same calmness she expressed in times of trouble.

"Mom, this is the long and short of it," Colin said in hurried speech.

Colin explained everything from the beginning of the day until they arrived home that evening. Sarah looked calm and her eyes shifted with keen interest between Colin and Benjamin as the story unfolded. There was no indication in her facial expression that she doubted anything. Her eyes revealed everything in her heart and soul.

"Colin, I believe you," she said with assurance. "I have never had a reason in my life to doubt you. Your daddy and I have always trusted in you. He often spoke about how the Lord had blessed him with the most precious gift from heaven above. He was so proud of you, Colin," she said with vigor but with eyes filled with tears.

"Thanks mom."

"Sarah, we need to act quickly. The events over the past few months are only the beginning of what is to come. We have only a few weeks to carry out our responsibility to those who will listen," Benjamin said with urgency.

"What do you need boys?" Count me in.

Chapter Nine

Sᴀʀᴀʜ ʜᴇᴀᴅᴇᴅ sᴏᴜᴛʜ ᴀʟᴏɴɢ highway 75 towards the county line.

News of the day's attack on America only fueled their determination to locate as many of the descendants of the people from below before things became worse.

"Eli told us we were to locate seventy descendants of his people and give them the knowledge to return to the world below," Colin explained. "These seventy will then be responsible to locate seventy more descendents until everyone has been found."

The small car she was driving had reached 72 mph and began to rattle with the increased speed. It was now after eleven o'clock at night but there were more cars on the highway than was usual for his time of night.

"You left out an important piece for our mission Colin," Benjamin added. "Our descendants are to meet in the central part of the United States in the town of Last Hope. Once there, they are to organize themselves and purchase property."

"That shouldn't be too hard to do since property values in that area have dropped below the national average. The economic prosperity once promised by government never came to fruition. Many in Last Hope have homes in foreclosure do to the corrupt mismanagement of home loans," explained Colin's mom.

The ride through the night was taking its toll on Sarah. She rolled the windows down to allow the warm air blow her hair. Colin and Benjamin knew they needed to continue talking to keep her from falling asleep at the wheel. Colin pulled from his backpack a flat stone with the inscribed names and location of the first seventy descendants. They lived within a 30 mile radius in the Lincoln County area just across the state border. Sarah had driven more than 280 miles in four hours on the road. The gas gage indicated less than a eighth of a tank left. They drove into Lincoln County just after two in the morning. The inscribed flat stone had 15 descendants living just north of Madison Avenue off of Main Street.

"Mom, turn left at the next intersection."

They drove for a two miles on Main Street and stopped near the home of the first descendant listed on the stone. There was no light coming from the home as Colin and Benjamin approached it. Sarah remained parked on the street out front.

"I'm a little nervous, aren't you?" Colin said with a slight quiver in his voice.

"There is nothing to fear when you put your trust in God. He will guide us as long as we remain obedient to Him. The world thought they could find solutions to their problems only relying on their reasoning. This worked for awhile but it failed them when they began to only trust in their own thinking," said Benjamin.

"You're right, I get that. I need to put more trust in God. I guess I am still new at this," Colin admitted.

"No, you have always had an open heart to listen and to follow. Unlike many in the world, your heart is still open to receive God's instruction for you. God knew he could count on you because of your obedient heart."

"I guess you're right. I don't mean that in an arrogant way. I just mean that I can recognize it better now," said Colin.

Colin and Benjamin walked up the front steps and stopped at the wooden door. Colin was the first to bang on the door. Benjamin followed with a second pounding. An interior light came on and its brightness beamed through a front window and onto the porch floor. Colin and Benjamin could hear a few muffled voices inside. They both could hear someone saying, "Shush" to the others inside. The front door flew open.

They were met with a bright light coming from a flashlight. The source of the light seemed to be coming from below them.

"Who are you?" came the voice of a small child.

"We're Colin and Benjamin and were looking for your mom and dad," Colin said.

Another voice sounded from behind the blinding light.

Why are you here?" asked a little girl not much older than six years of age as she stepped in front of the light.

"Like I said, we are here to talk to your mom and dad," Colin said anxiously. "What are your names?"

"I'm Ruthie," said the little girl.

"I'm David," said the young boy behind the flashlight.

"Look, we don't mean to scare you or cause you any harm. We just need to talk to your mom and dad. Can you get them for us?" said Colin.

"Mom! Dad!" hollered David.

A loud pounding on the floor above could be heard coming through the porch rafters. It wasn't much longer when a tall man stood in the doorway holding a baseball bat. Next to him, was a woman standing at shoulder height with the man next to her.

"What the heck is going on here?" the man said.

"I can explain everything sir," Benjamin stepped forward.

"With everything that has gone on today with the attack on the U.S. Capital building I hope you have a very good reason for knocking on our door at two o'clock in the morning," the man said with irritation.

"Sir, I know your name is Jacob and that you and your family are descendants of my people that live below the Earth. My father's name is Eli."

"Please, come on in boys," Jacob's voice softened. "My parents taught me that one day messengers would come from the world below to teach me additional knowledge."

Colin and Benjamin entered the home. The small home was modestly furnished with items that could be found at a garage sale. A scratched leather couch was anchored near the front wall of the home. Two wooden table chairs without seat cushions were placed in front of a coffee table that appeared to have a few gauges in it. The home was neat and orderly. Colin noticed several books on a nearby wooden bookshelf covering a range of topics – "The Geography of America before 1830" – "16th Century Explorers" – "Raising Happy Children in the 21st Century" – "Guide to Home Repairs" – "Famous Quotes From World Leaders" – "Religions of the World" and numerous other titles filled the shelves. Placed on the coffee table was a copy of the Holy Bible and another book entitled - "Reference Guide to Hebrew Words."

"I'm sorry boys, I didn't introduce myself. I'm Hannah. Can I get either of you something to drink?"

Both Colin and Benjamin nodded yes at the same time. Ruthie ran to the kitchen with excitement before Hannah could even take one step.

"I take it she doesn't mind being up this early," Colin said with a giggle.

"We don't get visitors much so she is excited to have company in the home," Hannah explained.

Benjamin shifted in his chair and asked if they could start with a prayer before going into the details of their visit.

"Absolutely, that would be wonderful," said Jacob. "Would you go ahead and offer it."

"I'd love to," said Benjamin.

"Ruthie, we're about to say a prayer, come join us please," Hannah announced.

Ruthie returned with two cups of lemonade and placed them on the coffee table. She immediately dropped to her knees, folded her arms and bowed her head.

After the prayer, Benjamin explained in detail the purpose for their visit and how Benjamin's father, Eli, was the keeper of the records in the world below. The families listened with keen interest and asked several questions about their role in finding others and help prepare them to leave for Last Hope.

The plan was now in motion. There was no turning back. Gathering the descendants of the world below had begun.

The prophesy written years ago and preserved by the house of Eli had been fulfilled –

Through the mouths of two witnesses I will reveal My truth to the scattered descendants. They shall gather together My hidden tribe and the scattered descendants and will bring them together for My wise

purpose. They shall become one people and many shall fear. For God will not be mocked. Earth's obedience never will waver. Man's disobedience to My creations will bring chaos among the elements of the Earth. They will not respond anymore in that day when Man's heart and obedience to Me is far from Me. Fires shall rage, drought will scorch the earth; storms from the deep will create turmoil among man. My wisdom will be taken from the earth and man shall be left without My guidance. The earth will moan and lands will tremble before Me. Man's solutions will not be Mine and many shall seek and will not find. I AM the God of the Earth and the Earth is obedient to Me only. When Man fails to seek My wisdom they will fail to find their solutions. I AM the God of the Earth and in all things I have placed my hand. I will gather together My hidden tribe in that day to prepare for My coming. They will be the last of the obedient. I will preserve them for their obedience. The last hope of mankind will be found in my hidden tribe. The Earth moans for man's obedience and they will turn from My Wisdom. Their eyes will be blind to the truth. Their hearts will be cold. Their own wisdom shall fail them in that day. I will be slow to hear them for man will not mock God. All of My creations from the beginning will know in the end that I AM HE that created them. They will hear my voice and know that I AM the great I AM. Fear will not be replaced with peace. For My Peace will be taken from the Earth. Man will seek peace in that day and will not find it. For they have rejected the True Peace of the Earth. I AM who I say I AM and will not be mocked in that day. I will build a defense for my hidden tribe for they will turn to ME and live. They will be spared from the turmoil that will haunt the hearts of the haughty and prideful. In that day many shall seek Me and I will be slow to hear their cries. Great marvels of My hand will appear in the sky in that day. For Great is My name. In that day many will turn to me for True Peace and I will be slow to hear their cries. The Great I AM will not be mocked.

Chapter Ten

Sᴀʀᴀʜ'ꜱ ꜱᴍᴀʟʟ ʀᴇᴅ ᴄᴀʀ moved through the night passing towns of various sizes. It had been nearly twenty-four hours since Colin had went to the beach to swim. The adrenaline rush was wearing off and exhaustion was once again taking its toll.

He desperately tried to stay awake for his mom who was having her own difficulties staying awake. Benjamin was sound asleep in the back seat. His body had not been accustomed to the intense heat and humidity above ground.

"Honey, we have got to stop and get some rest," Sarah said with a yawn. The sign said a rest area was 2 miles ahead."

"Ok, mom, but just for a little while. We have much to do and God will strengthen us for it," Colin assured her.

Colin awoke to the sounds of sirens coming from the highway.

The state trooper sped past in pursuit of something that was beyond Colin's vision. His mom was already awake listening to the news. Benjamin popped up from the back seat startled by the loud siren.

Sarah announced with a distant voice, "Jerusalem was attacked today, Colin."

"What!" Colin said in a high pitch tone.

"Reports coming out of Jerusalem said it was a little after eleven o'clock in the morning our time. That would have been about 6pm their time," she said with sadness.

"Who's responsible?" Benjamin asked from the back seat.

"No one has claimed responsibility," her voice sounded angry..

"Another terrorist attack in the world within 24 hours," Colin said.

"Things are happening fast aren't they," Sarah sounded alarmed for the first time.

"Sarah, we have to overcome our own fears. God does not create fear. We are promised that if we prepare we need not fear. Your son has been prepared, Sarah. Your son is fulfillment of prophesy. He has been chosen of God and will be protected," Benjamin said boldly.

"Thank you, Benjamin," she said with a warm smile.

Colin pulled some granola bars and bottled waters from his backpack. The three of them sat quietly listening to other news of the day. This time they listened with a different attitude.

The news was tragic in most cases. Hundreds of acres burned and destroyed in brush fires in the West. Three more tornadoes destroyed homes and property in the Midwest. Another hurricane was gaining strength in the Atlantic and had been upgraded to a category 3 hurricane. The United States had never seen such destruction in such a short time in her 200 year history. There was another oil spill in the Gulf leaking thousands of gallons of oil a day. The clean up from a similar oil spill only a few years back never came to any completion. It seemed as if man had run out of solutions to their own problems. Nature was no longer interested in waiting between manmade crises. Nature was in full fury and no so called experts or politicians seemed to have any answers.

"This is not the hand of God," Benjamin emphasized. "The elements are responding to the disobedience of man. The Earth is letting man have what it desires."

"Destruction?" Colin asked.

"Yes, destruction," continued Benjamin. "We are witnessing how the elements respond to man's chaos. God is a God of order and does not bring upon nations these destructive patterns. He is the creator of a perfect world. Everything has its place and purpose. When that purpose is disrupted because of man's disobedience, the elements can no longer act in the matter for which they were created. God has permitted these things to happen for His own wise purposes. All glory should be given to the God of our world. Man in his pride has tried to use the elements for their own purposes without giving thanks to the God who created the elements. Man has abused the elements for their own selfish gains. The Earth is no longer replenishing itself. It is self-destructing because man has self-destructed."

"Let's say a prayer," Colin offered. "I'll go ahead and say it." Colin continued, "Almighty God, our Father in Heaven, help us this day to do what you want us to do. Put in our hearts where we should go and how we are to get there. We ask for your protection and we are very much grateful to you for what you have given us. Amen"

"That was beautiful, Colin," Sarah said as her voice cracked. "Where did you learn to pray like that?"

"I don't know, mom, the words just came from my heart," Colin said sincerely.

After making several stops that day to the descendants of the world below, they filled the gas tank for the second time. It was after 4pm and the ominous clouds looked angry. Streaks of lightning could be seen in all directions. The skies roared with thunder.

"I have never seen anything like this in the world below," Benjamin said in awe. "Just incredible!"

"These storms can get pretty intense," Colin added.

The rain came down as if sheets of glass were breaking from the windows of heaven. Small hail stones had now turned into golf ball size hail.

"I've got to stop, I can't see in front of me," Sarah sounding somewhat panicked.

"There is a bridge just up ahead," Benjamin said with excitement.

The car slowly moved forward at a snail's pace until it was underneath an underpass. The shear of water fell from the road top above and looked like they were sitting behind a waterfall.

Suddenly, a small board from a nearby lumber truck crashed through the windshield. Colin felt a warm, stinging sensation on the right side of his eye. He noticed Benjamin lay crouched behind Sarah's seat looking nervous for the first time they had known each other. Sarah quickly wiped some glass off of her lap and reached for some napkins out of her purse.

"Colin, your eye!" She said with astonishment.

Colin's right side of his eye socket appeared to be severely damaged. A piece of the small board struck him on the orbital bone and was now lodged. There was a gash in Colin's cheek where the small piece of wood had pierced his skin.

"I'm alright," Colin assured her. "I can see fine and I don't feel any pain."

"Benjamin, can you grab the first aid kit from the trunk? I usually keep it up front but tossed it there the other day while cleaning things out of the glove compartment," Sarah requested.

"No problem."

Benjamin had trouble opening the side door as the winds picked up speed and the gusts were increasingly stronger. Benjamin could hear the trunk pop ajar before he left the vehicle.

"Be careful out there. The winds are really strong." Colin looked back with a confident smile.

"I will," assured Benjamin.

Benjamin closed the door behind him and his shadow could be seen through the fogged windows.

"We'll wait it out under this bridge until the storm subsides," Sarah sounded worried.

"Hopefully it won't be much longer," Colin said with exasperation.

Colin heard the knock on the passenger side window. He could see the shadowy figure of Benjamin. Colin reached for the latch to open the door when another strong gust of wind broke away loose glass from the windshield. The impact of the gust left a gaping hole in the center of the windshield. Small pieces of glass were strewn throughout the car. To his surprise neither he nor his mom had been touched by this last barrage.

"That was close, mom," Colin said.

"Colin," Sarah said with heightened alarm. "He's gone. Benjamin is gone."

Colin quickly turned his head to where Benjamin had stood just moments before. He rotated his body peering through every inch of window. He could see nothing but a wall of water on both sides of the bridge.

"I'm going after him, mom"

"Colin, wait!" she pleaded.

"I can't. Benjamin is out there. I wouldn't be here if it wasn't for him," he retorted.

The door open and closed before she could utter another word. The wind howled through the open glass as water sprayed the interior.

"Please God, I know you hear me. Watch over my son and help him find Benjamin," she said softly from her quivering lips.

Chapter Eleven

COLIN LEANED FORWARD INTO the pelting rain. The wind seemed to push him back two steps for every step he took.

"Benjamin!" Colin screamed.

Colin walked near the side of the highway where the tall grass bent sideways do to the wind's force. Colin felt desperation as the storm raged above.

"Benjamin!" he yelled again from the top of his lungs.

The sound of his voice could not travel far with the howling wind. He squinted through the slashing rain to find a trace of Benjamin. Colin tripped over an object lying on the side of the road. He looked down at the tennis shoe Benjamin had worn that day. He bent down to pick up the shoe and saw Benjamin lying face down in the tall grass. He appeared unconscious.

Without hesitation Colin bent down and placed his arms underneath Benjamin's limp body. His body was covered with wet grass and mud but felt warm to the touch. Colin struggled to lift Benjamin. He was used to hauling stacks of hay into their old pick-up truck but the wind and rain were adding to the burden.

"Please God, I need strength to carry Benjamin back to the car," Colin cried aloud.

Without warning, the rain suddenly subsided. The wind that was roaring moments ago was now a soft breeze.

Colin thanked God in his mind and carried Benjamin back to the car.

He had only walked a distance of about fifty feet from the car but it seemed a lot further in the wind and rain.

The passenger door flew open.

"Thank God in Heaven, you're both okay," Sarah shouted with gratitude.

"I'm fine mom but I'm not so certain about Benjamin."

They laid Benjamin on his back in the rear seat.

"He's got a pulse and his blood pressure is fine," Sarah said.

"Thank God," Colin whispered aloud.

"He will be fine, Colin. He will be fine," she assured him.

They both retreated to the front seat and allowed their bodies to sink into the cushioned seats. In minutes they were sound asleep as exhaustion consumed their bodies' ability to stay awake. High up above the bridge and unknown to Colin, Sarah, and Benjamin hovered a towering rainbow. The dark clouds had dissipated and were replaced with a blue sky above. Three hours had passed since the storm began and Benjamin was the first to awake from his deep sleep.

"Sarah, Colin, are you okay?"

"I was until you woke me," Colin said in a happy, sarcastic tone. "Benjamin, I'm the one who should be asking are you okay."

"How is your head, Benjamin?" Sarah asked in a comforting tone.

"I have a little headache, but other than that I am fine," Benjamin affirmed. "But I would be more worried about Colin's wound."

"I'm fine, believe it or not. That obnoxious splinter must have ripped out when I went to search for you. I can't believe it. Even the blood is dry where the small piece of wood entered my cheek," Colin said in a relieved manner.

"God is indeed watching over us," Sarah said with praise.

"Amen to that," Colin confirmed.

"How far is it to Last Hope, Sarah?" Benjamin asked.

"According to the GPS, we have about another six hundred miles to go or about ten more hours on the road," Sarah responded.

"We've got to get to Last Hope by tomorrow morning," Benjamin announced. "We must arrive ahead of any descendants that will be arriving over the next several days and weeks ahead."

"I'm ready if you boys are ready," Sarah said with enthusiasm.

"Let's roll," Colin said remembering the last words of a heroic American from the 911 attack.

Chapter Twelve

THE NEWS FROM WASHINGTON was grim as the small car rolled along towards Last Hope. Two more attacks on Jerusalem were carried out by extremists. The Statue of Liberty was damaged the same day by a small explosion which tore portions of plated copper from the base of Lady Liberty. Radio news reported that the damage was minimal and could be repaired in a few weeks.

Colin couldn't imagine anything ever happening to the Statue of Liberty. She was the symbol of freedom to the rest of the world. She represented all that was good about America and its people. 'This couldn't be the end of our great nation,' Colin thought to himself. He remembered the stories that his Great-Grandfather Jack told about the courage and sacrifice of the soldiers who fought in World War II. His Grand-Father Luke shared with him the horrors of Vietnam but how men valiantly sacrificed themselves for their friends in combat.

He thought deep into the night remembering all that was good about America. American meant freedom from tyranny as promised in the Declaration of Independence. It meant the pursuit of happiness and having the liberty to pursue your own dreams. The United States Constitution spoke of a more perfect union, domestic tranquility, and for the common **defence**. He wondered if America could ever regain her glory that was once the envy of the world.

He remembered his Uncle Tim coming home from wars in the Middle East talking about the positive influence American Soldiers had made on the people in those countries. So much had been sacrificed. So much blood had been spilled on foreign and domestic soil. Many young men and women died, so others whom they knew not, could have freedom to live according to the dictates of their own minds. He believed they did this so others could be free from oppressive governments and could worship God in their own way and possibly raise families so future generations could prosper. Colin remembered all that was good about the America he read about and his ancestors that were now part of the American fabric of those who died for something greater than themselves.

The heavens opened up for America throughout history and Colin was convinced of that now. God was the director of her fate and He was counting on courageous men and women to renew their commitment to the God of Abraham and find it within themselves to rededicate their time, talents, and energies to serving mankind. Colin knew that obedience to the God of this world was the only solution to the Earth's troubles. What he didn't know is if the earth's elements could respond once again to man's willingness to change their ways. He didn't know what lay ahead for America or the world.

The little red car sputtered into a gas station early the next morning around 6am. The three of them got out from the vehicle and released the soreness with pulls and stretches. A gas station attendant came out in blue overhauls wiping his hands of grease and said, "Hi all, aint it good to be alive and well in Last Hope, America. Why it is good to see folks coming into town with everyone leaving here due to the housing market."

"Oh, it is so good to be here," Sarah said with a bright smile.

"Aint that the truth," said Colin.

"Amen to that," added Benjamin.

There was so much uncertainty in the days that lie ahead. Descendants of the world below would be arriving over the next few weeks, and only God knew what was expected of Colin when they did arrive.

The preparation was just beginning. They would make a new home in Last Hope and work to rebuild a city that from the look of it was desolate. Homes were in disrepair. Roads and bridges had been neglected for years. Church steeples had been weathered by the seasons, and paint chips littered the ground beneath them.

Colin looked over his left shoulder and could feel the sun rising from the east. A small radio resting on an old rusted chair next to a pop machine echoed the morning news.

"Good morning America, later today the President of the United States is expected to ask congress to reinstate the "National Day of Prayer" that had been rejected by Congress over a decade ago. The President said this was in large measure do to the catastrophic weather events and the recent terrorist attacks on American soil and in Jerusalem…."

The sun felt good on Colin's battered cheek. Benjamin looked over at Colin from across the small gas station lot. Benjamin picked a flyer from the trash can next to the gas pump.

"It says here that homes and farmland are for sale at Sheriff's auction prices," Benjamin shared with a wide grin.

"Well, what do you think, mom?"

"Why not, let's take a look and see what God has in store for us," she said with tearful laughter.

"Could we say a prayer first before we head on," said Colin.

"Well, I haven't heard one of those in years," said the gas station attendant somewhat shamefully.

"Would you say one for us," Benjamin requested.

"Sure thing, why not," said the gas station attendant.

Colin bowed his head and folded his arms. Before he closed his eyes, he noticed another rainbow coming from the Northeast. 'How unusual,' he thought to himself. 'There isn't a rain cloud in the sky.'

Colin caught Benjamin glancing over at him with a smile on his face. Somehow Colin knew that the rainbow was not by accident or some freak of nature. Colin felt inside that maybe, just maybe, the elements were responding to the prayer of the gas station attendant. With his head uncovered from this greasy cap, the gas station attendant continued his prayer.

"Our great God in heaven above, may we give thanks for this beautiful morning and for these new comers. May this great land be protected by your hand and may these fine people find peace in Last Hope. This I pray. Amen"

"Amen to that," all three said simultaneously.

"Mom, what are we going to do about our house back home?" Colin asked.

"I think our last move was a lot harder to make than this one.

We've done it before and we can do it again," said Sarah

They hopped back into their small car and thanked the gas station attendant for his sincere prayer. They drove slowly passed several vacant homes and businesses. Last Hope didn't look like it offered much hope for anyone looking to start their lives over again. However, there seemed to be a peacefulness that settled over the city. In the next few days and weeks ahead, descendants of the world below, would make Last Hope their new home.

One people with one purpose would soon occupy the vacancy that now existed. Last Hope represented to America now what Bunker Hill or The Alamo represented to America's great past. It would soon be made up of those willing to take the last stand for all that America represented to itself and the rest of the world. It would require the next generation of God fearing individuals who understood that Divine Providence had his hand in America's former greatness and required a people that would turn to Him again for protection and prosperity. If that could happen, then just maybe, America and the world had one last hope for humanity.

Epilogue

As Colin peddled down Patrick Henry Street, the thought occurred to him that he should turn back, and say goodbye to Benjamin one last time. It wouldn't have surprised him if he did. But he didn't. He kept going resisting the temptation and pedaled faster. He leaned into the wind and looked ahead into the distance. His course was now set and he knew what he had to do. He had already said goodbye to Benjamin moments ago and saying it again would only make the task for the both of them that much harder. Benjamin had to return to his father, Eli, and give him a report. He would be needed in the world below to prepare the people for their return to the world above.

New citizens arrived daily to Last Hope. The journey for many of them had not been easy. They had sold their homes and many of their belongings to begin anew in a city they had never known. They purchased dilapidated homes and began to refurbish them. They brought their professional and manual labor skills to create a shining light for the rest of the country to admire. Schools were organized. Prayer was a part of the daily experience before the Pledge of Allegiance was recited. Streets were cleaned and lined with newly planted trees. Small business owners worked with local banks to create an economy based on basic principles of thrift, industry, honesty, trust, and concern for the individual community member.

The transition wasn't easy for those arriving to Last Hope but smoother than Colin expected it to be. He was amazed at the descendants of the world below. They had lived separated for years in various parts of the country and yet they came with the same spirit of oneness and purpose. Last Hope was slowly but surely taking shape as a model city for the rest of America, and for that matter, the rest of the world.

This was no utopia in the traditional sense of the word. This city was being transfigured through the inspiration of the Almighty himself and not left up to man. Individuals retained their property rights and were expected to work an honest living to provide for their own.

A little over a decade ago, Last Hope had a population of a little over 15,000 thousand people. However, after several years, the population dwindled to fewer than one thousand residents due to the poor economic recovery. Some of those would stay and integrate themselves with the new arrivals. Most, however, wanted nothing to do with the new citizens of Last Hope and left to make a new home elsewhere.

Colin and his mom settled into a small one story two bedroom home just on the outskirts of town. Sarah began working full-time at one of the local banks and Colin started school in the fall. Colin knew the troubles facing America were not going to improve unless Benjamin returned with his father and the people from the world below. Colin was counting on it and reuniting with them was America's last hope if she were to survive as a nation. If America didn't survive, then the world would not be able to withstand the catastrophic events that would continue to haunt the planet until all forms of life became extinct.